The ADVENTURES of "CHUCK E. BEAVER" AND FRIENDS

THE NEW BIKE

Written by
Kiki

Illustrated by
SOUSOU YERETSIAN

Published by
Montbec Inc.

Publisher
MATT ARENY

Publication Advisor
JOSE AZEVEDO

Editorial Supervisor
ETHEL SALTZMAN

Artwork Supervisor
PIERRE RENAUD

ISBN 2-89227-224-6

THE NEW BIKE

For Chuck E.'s seventh birthday,
Mr. and Mrs. Beaver got him a brand new
bicycle. Chuck E. was so happy. He had
dreamed many times of owning a bike
like this one. Every time he and his
parents had passed by the bicycle store,
he always stopped and went inside to
have a look at it. Now it was his, and he
had to make sure nothing happened to it.

Chuck E. spent a lot of time cleaning his new bike. When he got home from school, he would rush out to the garage to make sure his bike was still there. He took very good care of it and his parents were proud of him.

"Son, I'm happy to see you're keeping your bike looking new!" Mr. Beaver remarked, as he saw Chuck E. in the driveway polishing his bike.

"Thanks, Pop!" Chuck E. replied.
"I love my new bike and I want it to look
clean and shiny all the time!"

"Well, that's good, son. It's always very
important to look after your things, so
that nothing happens to them. It shows
that you're responsible and that you
appreciate them."

"Well, I certainly appreciate you and
Mom buying me this new bike, Pop,"
Chuck E. beamed. "I'll never let anything
bad happen to it!"

"I'm glad to hear that son," Mr. Beaver smiled back, "because it would be very hard to replace. Now, remember, never leave it without locking it up, okay?"

"I won't, Pop!" Chuck E. assured his father. "Pop, may I ride my bike down to the park with Bobby after school today?"

"Sure, son, as long as you bring your lock with you," Mr. Beaver agreed.

"Thanks, Pop!" Chuck E. said happily.

After school, Bobby agreed to meet Chuck E. at his house so they could ride their bikes down to the park.

"Say, Chuck E., that sure is a nice bike!" Bobby complimented Chuck E. "It still looks brand new!"

"Well, I take very good care of it," Chuck E. told him. "I polish it every day when I get home from school."

"It really shines!" Bobby exclaimed.

"Are you ready to head down to the park?" Bobby asked, as he jumped on his bike.

"You bet!" Chuck E. replied enthusiastically. "Just let me get my lock first and then we'll head off!"

"Why do you need your lock?" Bobby asked. "We won't be leaving our bikes anywhere."

"Well, my father told me not to leave my bike anywhere without locking it up," Chuck E. explained, "but I guess if we don't leave them I don't really need it."

"Okay, then, let's go!" Bobby said, as
he started off down the driveway.

"I'm right behind you!" Chuck E. called.

18

At the park Chuck E. and Bobby rode along the bicycle path that wound through it, until they arrived at the end where the snack bar was. The boys stopped and got off their bikes for a moment.

"Say, Chuck E.," Bobby said, "I've got some money left over from my allowance. Do you want to go in and get a couple of hot dogs?"

"Sure!" Chuck E. replied excitedly as he thought about biting into a big tasty hot dog, "but what about the bikes? We can't leave them alone out here without a lock!"

"Oh, they'll be alright!" Bobby assured him. "We'll only be a minute. What could possibly happen to them in a minute?" he asked.

"I guess you're right," Chuck E. agreed. "One minute should be okay. Let's go!"

Bobby was very happy. He put his arm around Chuck E.'s neck and they went in.

Chuck E. and Bobby were inside for only a couple of minutes. They went out chomping on their hot dogs. They walked over to where they had left their bikes, but Chuck E.'s was nowhere in sight.

"Oh, no!" Chuck E. exclaimed in shock. "Where's my bike?" He looked around in every direction.

"Now calm down, Chuck E.," Bobby tried to help his friend. "It's got to be here somewhere!"

The two of them looked frantically around the building, but they couldn't see the bike anywhere. In a half hour, it started to get dark out, and it was very difficult to see.

"Chuck E., I think we'd better start heading home now," Bobby suggested. "It's getting late and my mom will start worrying."

"How can I go home without my bike?" Chuck E. asked, looking very upset. "My father is going to be very angry if he finds out I lost my bike!"

"He'll be angrier if you don't get home before it gets dark!" Bobby said. "Anyway there isn't anything else that we can do now," he added.

"I guess you're right, Bobby," Chuck E. finally said, "but will you come in with me and help me explain what happened?"

"Okay, if you think it will help," Bobby agreed.

In order to get home quickly, Chuck E. sat on Bobby's crossbar and they rode home on one bike. As they got to the house, Mr. Beaver was just driving up. He stopped his car and saw Chuck E. sitting on Bobby's crossbar.

"Chuck E!" Mr. Beaver exclaimed, "why are you riding on Bobby's crossbar when you know you're not supposed to?"

"I-I'm sorry, Dad," Chuck E. apologized, "but I have an explanation."

"By the way, I don't seem to see your bike anywhere," Mr. Beaver went on. "Is it in the garage already?"

"Well-er, no," Chuck E. stammered.

"Well, then, can you tell me where it is?" Mr. Beaver continued.

"Well, you see, that's part of the whole story," Chuck E. said nervously.

"I think we'd all better go inside, so you can tell me what's going on," Mr. Beaver suggested.

Mr. Beaver told the boys to sit down in the living room. He asked Mrs. Beaver to call Bobby's parents to let them know that Bobby was at their house.

"Now, who's going to start?" Mr. Beaver asked, as he sat down beside the boys.

"I guess I'd better," Chuck E. said.

Chuck E. told his father about the trip to the park, and what happened after he and Bobby came out of the snack bar. By the time Chuck E. had finished his story, Mr. Beaver looked quite upset.

"I'm very disappointed in you, Chuck E.," Mr. Beaver commented. "I told you just this morning not to leave your bike anywhere without locking it, didn't I?"

"Yes, Pop, you did, and I'm very ashamed of myself," Chuck E. confessed. "But what can we do now about my bike?"

"Well, all we can do is call the Police Department and hope that it turns up," Mr. Beaver answered. "But it may never be found.

"I hope the police can find it," Chuck E. said, with tears in his eyes.

"Well, let's hope so," Mr. Beaver added, giving Chuck E. a hug, "but why don't we go down to the park tomorrow and see if we can find it ourselves, okay?"

"Do you mean it, Pop?" Chuck E. asked eagerly. "I'm sure it will be there! I know it will!"

"We can only hope, son," Mr. Beaver said. "Now you two go into the kitchen and get yourselves something to eat."

Mr. Beaver called the Police Department to report Chuck E.'s stolen bike, and they agreed to look for it. The next day, Mr. Beaver picked up Chuck E. and Bobby at school, and they headed down to the park. As they were driving along the park road just before the snack bar, they noticed something shiny in the bushes beside the road.

"Hey, did you see that?" Chuck E. shouted as he pointed to the glitter.

"Yes, son, I see it, too! Let's stop and have a look," Mr. Beaver suggested.

Chuck E. and Bobby quickly jumped out of the car and bolted over to where the shine was coming from. As they got closer to the bushes, they noticed a bicycle wheel sticking out. Mr. Beaver came running up to give them a hand.

"Dad! Dad! It's here!" Chuck E. shouted with joy. "It's my bike! It's got to be!"

"Well, let's have a look, son," Mr. Beaver said, as he pushed the branches to one side. Then they saw the rest of Chuck E.'s bike. Mr. Beaver lifted it out and placed it on the road, to the delight of both Chuck E. and Bobby.

"Wow, Chuck E!" Bobby cried, "you're so lucky!"

"I know," Chuck E. said, heaving a big sigh of relief. "But why would someone just throw it in these bushes, instead of bringing it back where it was?" he wondered.

43

"Well, son, I guess whoever took your
bike was afraid of returning it, because
they thought they might get caught,"
Mr. Beaver tried to explain. "Let's just be
thankful that it was returned and that it's
okay."

"I really am!" Chuck E. replied happily.
"And I'm never going to leave my bike
anywhere without locking it first from
now on. Not even for one minute!" he
promised.

"Me neither!" Bobby agreed.

"Well, I hope so," Mr. Beaver
commented, "because the next time you
may not be so fortunate."

Chuck E. and Bobby made sure there
was no next time. After this close call,
they never let their bikes out of their
sight, unless they were securely locked.

Take care of your things

And don't leave them unprotected.

Thefts and accidents can happen

When they're least expected.

Your friend,

Chuck E.